MW01034249

IRISH CRIME

True Crime Stories

True Crime Books
Series - Book 2

Roger Harrington

Copyright © 2017.

All rights reserved. No part of this
publication may be reproduced, distributed,
or transmitted in any form or by any means,
including photocopying, recording, or other
electronic or mechanical methods, without
the prior written permission of the publisher,
except in the case of brief quotations
embodied in critical reviews and certain
other noncommercial uses permitted by
copyright law.

This book is intended for informational and
entertainment purposes only. The publisher
limits all liability arising from this work to
the fullest extent of the law.

Table of Contents

Chapter 1

Ireland has a long history of crime and passion. Their national identity has been forged from the blood of war, one war that brought the nation its freedom and another that literally split the country in two.

Ireland's healing process has been promising but slow. Though many old wounds still cut deep into the lives of its citizens, Ireland today is known for its friendly and vibrant culture. But even the most peaceful locales can play host to some of the world's most vicious crimes.

Chapter 2

On April 20, 1954, Michael Manning, a convicted murderer, became the final person to be executed in the Republic of Ireland. Manning was the last in a line of men and women, many of whom died fighting for Irish nationalism in the early 1900's.

Michael Manning was 25 years old in 1954, the year he raped and murdered a 65-year-old nurse while drunk one cold February night in Limerick. Manning worked long hours as a carter, someone who operated an animal-drawn cart in to transport goods around their city. The job wasn't great, but he needed it to support his heavily pregnant wife. In the Irish tradition, Manning was also a heavy drinker. He would later blame his drinking for his own heinous crime.

One fateful evening, Manning was returning home to his pregnant wife after a day's drinking when he saw a woman he did not recognize. The woman was Catherine Cooper, a 65-year-old nurse who was also returning home from Barrington's Hospital where she worked. She was walking across the street from Manning after a hard day's work saving lives.

When Manning spotted Cooper across the street, something inside him snapped. They were both alone on the dark street, the perfect opportunity for crime. Manning ran across the road and ambushed the old nurse with a physical assault. It was easy for the young, fit man to overpower Cooper, and he had her on the ground in no time. Once she was incapacitated, Manning shoved handfuls of grass into Cooper's mouth to prevent her from screaming. He then proceeded to sexually assault and rape Cooper, stopping only when the lights of a passing car shone on him. Cooper died during the attack.

Manning quickly ran off, but his inebriated state prevented him from making much ground. The driver of the car that had witnessed Manning attacking Cooper was quick to call police. Manning was arrested within hours of his crime.

When he was questioned by police, Manning admitted to raping Catherine Cooper. When confronted with the fact that she had died during the attack, Manning denied that murder was his intention, stating that something simply broke in his mind and he couldn't remember anything between the time he crossed the road and ran off. It he had killed Cooper; it was because he drank too much. He hadn't meant to do a thing.

Manning's case quickly went to trial. During his trial, Manning again admitted to committing the sexual assault that had led to Cooper's death, but insisted he couldn't be held accountable for his actions as he was drunk at the time and had a history of mental health issues. When it was clear to him that this excuse wasn't going to buy him his freedom, he apologized vehemently.

Despite receiving pleas from both Manning and Cooper's families, the judge presiding over Manning's trial sentenced him to death for his crimes by hanging. An execution by hanging was legal at the time in Ireland and was the standard sentence by law for murder. The judge had little choice in the matter, and had also stated his own belief that Manning should be held fully accountable for his actions. Manning had been aware enough to shove grass into his victim's mouth in an attempt to keep her quiet; he was not acting simply out of a drunken stupor.

The Irish media at the time painted Manning as a monster; he was a brutish man who had killed an elderly nurse, someone who had dedicated their entire life to helping others.

However, those who were around Manning while he was waiting to be executed said the man was actually far from monsters. He spent most of the time in his cell smoking cigarettes and reading the local newspaper. He regularly attended mass, and both he and his wife often thanked the prison staff for their kindness towards both of them.

Michael Manning's execution took place within two months of the night he murdered Catherine Cooper. Just before 8am on April 20th, 1954, Manning was escorted to the Mountjoy Prison hanghouse in Dublin, a site that is preserved to this day. His wrists and legs were bound and a linen hood was placed over his head before the fatal noose. When the oak trap doors of the gallows opened, Manning dropped to his instantaneous death.

Manning was buried in one of the many unmarked graves behind the Mountjoy prison. Ten years after Manning hung, the death penalty became illegal in Ireland except in cases involving treason or the murder of police or diplomats. In this ten-year span, eleven people were sentenced to executions, but all had their sentences commuted by the Irish Prime Minister. In 1990, the death penalty was abolished completely.

Chapter 3

When the Criminal Justice Act of 1990 abolished the death penalty for good in, it was the end of one of Ireland's bloodiest chapters of history. Although only about 30 prisoners were hung between 1923 and 1954, executions had played a significant role in the Irish's fight for independence from British rule.

The most infamous case of executions in Ireland was the executions by firing squad of the Easter Rising leaders in 1916. The Easter Rising was a hostile rebellion that was launched by Irish republicans in a bid to end British rule in the country. The Rising lasted six days and took 485 lives of both military men and civilians.

On April 24, 1916, members of the Irish Citizen Army and the Irish Volunteers seized key prominent buildings throughout the city of Dublin and declared an Independent Irish Republic. They built blockades and defended their territory with firearms. There was fierce street fighting throughout the city center, and many casualties were taken on both sides. The British Army responded to the crisis by bringing in thousands of reinforcements, all heavily armed.

Initially, the response towards the Irish rebels was negative amongst the Irish civilians. The Citizen Army was seen as overly radical and the fighting had taken over the streets of the entire city. Many citizens were trapped in their houses altogether, and several civilians were shot in their own homes simply because they lived near an area with a lot of activity. Of the nearly 500 people who died in the Rising, about 54% were civilians.

After six solid days of fighting, the Easter Rising finally came to an end. The British army declared victory. They had much greater numbers and resources and had heavier weapons than the rebels. Although the Irish rebels were willing to die for their cause, and many did, they eventually had to face the fact that they could not possibly continue to hold their territories for much longer. An unconditional surrender was signed on April 29, 1916 by Patrick Pearse, a prominent leader of the rising who had been a school teacher before joining the Irish Citizen Army.

Public opinion on the Rising slowly began to change after the surrender of the rebels. When more information was made available, it became clear that most of the civilian casualties had been at the hands of the British Army, not the Irish rebels. The British Army had used heavy machine guns in heavily built-up areas, which destroyed anything in its path, be it a rebel barricade or civilian home. They also used incendiary shells, ammunition designed to light everything it touched on fire.

Most damningly in the public's eyes though, the British Army had shot many civilians point-blank in the chance that they may have been aiding the rebels, or been rebels themselves. This inability to discern rebels from civilians, or the lack of effort to, made many Irish citizens feel like Britain had been more concerned with their own interests in maintaining control of Ireland than respecting or protecting Irish lives—a sentiment that had a deep sting amongst many who remembered the horrors of the Irish potato famine.

By May of 1916, public opinion on the Easter Rising had completely switched. When all the leaders of the Rising were sentenced to death, and some of the horrific details surrounding the executions were released, many Irish civilians firmly felt that the British government and army had little to no regard for Irish life.

Between May 3 and May 12, fourteen individuals who were determined to be involved in the Rising were executed by firing squad, despite only seven of these men having signed the Proclamation of Irish Independence that was distributed during the Rising. There were many questions raised about the need to execute the seven other men.

The execution of three men in particular led to a major outcry. John MacBride and Thomas Kent were both executed on May 5 despite neither of them participating in the Rising itself. MacBride claimed he was not aware of the Rising until it had begun, but he had fought against the British in the Boer War fifteen years prior, which was enough justification for the British. Kent, however, had killed a police officer, but it was during a violent raid on his home a week after the

Rising. He stated he had acted out of self-defense and in fear of his family's safety. He had no connection to the Rising or the Irish Citizen Army.

James Connolly's execution on May 12 was seen as the most brutal of the fourteen. Connolly had been heavily involved in the Rising, and had since been declared a hero in the eyes of the Irish along with many of his cohorts. Connolly had been severely injured in Rising. Amongst his injuries, he had shattered his ankle, leaving him unable to stand. For his execution, Connolly was tied to a chair and then shot. It was a bloody image that helped the Irish sees him as a helpless martyr who had died trying to free the helpless Irish from the overpowering British rule.

These executions marked the end of the Easter Rising in Ireland, but the actions of the Irish rebels had a lasting imprint in Ireland that eventually led to the country being granted what the rebels had been fighting for — an independent Irish state.

Chapter 4

While the Easter Rising ultimately succeeded in its purpose of freeing the Irish from British rule, the country would have to face many more terrors before finally finding peace. One of these terrors was the Dublin and Monaghan car bombings.

The Dublin and Monaghan car bombings were a series of coordinated bombings that took place in both Dublin and Monaghan, Ireland. The bombings killed 33 civilians, marking them as the deadliest attack of the Troubles in Northern Ireland and the Republic of Ireland's history.

In the 1970's, Northern Ireland was in the middle of a political and nationalistic guerrilla war that was being fought by its own citizens. Violence and murder was a daily occurrence in the larger cities of Derry and Belfast. Although the Republic of Ireland was settling into its new status as a free nation, many in Northern Ireland were still struggling with their identities and what it meant to be Northern Irish. Without a clear sense of self, those living in Northern Ireland lashed out. Altogether, over 3,600 people were killed and thousands more were injured over the 30 year period commonly referred to as the Troubles.

For those living in Dublin, 100 miles South of Belfast, it was easy to forget the madness that was happening up North. Dublin had seen its fair share of violence over the years, and the city was finally prospering after years of its own hardships. That abruptly came to an end on May 17, 1974.

It was rush hour on a Friday evening when the first bomb exploded without warning in Dublin. The first bomb exploded at 5:30pm exactly on Talbot Street, a significant street in Dublin's history that bears a remembrance plaque for Sean Treacy, a prominent Irish Republican who was shot during the War of Independence.

The car bearing the first bomb was parked on the street outside a Pub and a Supermarket. It was a metallic green 1970 Hillman Avenger. When the bomb exploded, it hurled a brown Mini that had been parked behind the bomb towards innocent bystanders. Ten people were killed in the explosion.

A second bomb detonated on Parnell Street, a street also steeped in history. Parnell Street had once been named Great Britain Street, but had been renamed following the War of Independence. Its namesake was Charles Parnell, an Irish nationalist politician who had become leader of the Home Rule League in 1880.

This second bomb had been loaded into a metallic blue Ford Escort that was strategically parked alongside the main route between the Dublin city center and the populated railway station, Connolly station. The explosion killed twelve people on the spot, and two more died over the following few days. Thirteen of the fourteen victims were women, one woman of whom was nine months pregnant at the time.

A third bomb was detonated on South Leinster Street. This time, the bomb had been carried by a blue Austin 1800 Maxi parked outside of Trinity College. Two women were killed by the blast and many others were injured. Dental students from the College rushed to the scene to give first aid after witnessing the blast.

Within 90 seconds central Dublin was devastated. Witnesses recalled seeing victims who no longer had faces. One witness described seeing a young girl that he initially mistook for a rag doll torn to pieces. It was a scene from a war movie—decapitated corpses lay in the middle of the road entangled with one another. All around, bystanders watched the life trickle out of their friends, neighbors, and relatives.

Twenty-six people were killed in Dublin that day, and 253 were injured.

Ninety minutes after the Dublin explosions, a fourth bomb went off in Monaghan, a town just south of the Northern Ireland border. Monaghan is a much smaller city than Dublin, but the explosion's aftermath was no less deadly.

The Monaghan bomb was implanted in a green Hillman Minx that was parked outside a Protestant-owned pub on the city's North Road. It was also approximately 400 yards away from a police station. Witnesses were able to later tell police that the car had only parked in the spot within five minutes of the explosion happening. It is likely that the police station had been the intended target, but the bombers were unable to park close enough in time. The explosion killed five people the day of and two more in hospital during the following weeks.

Security forces from the border were called down to help deal with the hectic scene that now plagued Monaghan's streets. It is widely believed that those responsible for the Dublin bombings had intended this to happen in order to make it easier for them to escape back across the border to Belfast, where they were from.

Chapter 5

During the four explosions, 33 people altogether were killed, and nearly 300 were injured. It was the worst atrocity of the Troubles. More disturbingly, to this day, no one person or party has been convicted for taking part in these terrible bombings. In fact, many, except for those who lived in Dublin at the time, have forgotten the bombings happened at all.

The Irish police carried out the official investigation into the bombings in the biggest murder manhunt that has ever taken place in Ireland. Although no one has ever been convicted of any crimes in relation to the bombings, within weeks of them happening the Irish police knew the identities of the men who carried out the bombings, as well as how they managed to carry out the bombings. At the time, unfortunately, the Irish police were powerless to do anything about it.

The bombing mission started in Belfast on May 15, 1974. Two cars were hijacked in the Protestant Shankill neighborhood and a third was stolen from a nearby residence. They were later identified as the three Dublin car bomb wrecks.

The Belfast hijackers headed south to deliver the cars to members of a car bomb gang, who often rigged cars for deadly explosions in Northern Ireland. The hijackers and the car bombers met up in an abandoned farmhouse just North of where Monaghan hits the

Northern Irish border. Here, the cars were stored until they were properly rigged up and ready to cause havoc.

When all three of the cars were ready to roll, they were taken down to Dublin separately. The Dublin bomb cars managed to get across the border unchecked as those driving them used an unapproved border crossing that was part of an old smuggler's trail. The cars kept to the backroads until they reached their final destination. During their investigation, the police uncovered eye witnesses who could remember seeing the cars on their journey to Dublin that fateful day.

By 4pm on May 17, 1974, all three cars had gathered together in a parking lot on the outskirts of Dublin. Here, they primed the bombs and waited until the right moment to leave for their intended targets.

Meanwhile, the Monaghan bombers waited until the day of the 17th to steal a car from a parking lot in Portadown, Northern Ireland. Three men were involved in this car theft, and all three men were later identified by a Minister who had seen them attempting to steal a different car earlier that day. All three men were prominent loyalist terrorists from Portadown.

After the Monaghan bombers successfully secured themselves a car, they drove it to its fateful destination, stopping only briefly in the same farmhouse as the Dublin bombers to pick up their explosive devices. The men then used a different smuggler's trail to illegally cross the border. They were closely followed by another vehicle, which would serve as their getaway car.

Altogether, eight different men were identified by eyewitnesses for either driving one of the cars that later exploded, or for driving one of the suspected getaway vehicles. All eight men were members of the UVF, the Ulster Volunteer Force, which was a loyalist paramilitary group that operated out of Northern Ireland.

During the height of its activity, the UVF was classified as a terrorist organization by the United Kingdom, the Republic of Ireland, and the United States. The group took up an armed campaign for almost thirty years during Northern Ireland's Troubles. Although the group signed a ceasefire in 1994, it didn't officially end its campaign to combat Irish republicanism until 2007.

The main goal of the UVF was to maintain Northern Ireland's status as part of the United Kingdom. To do this, the group waged a war on everyone they felt opposed or didn't belong in their territory. Altogether, the group was directly responsible for more than 500 deaths through their deadly demonstrations.

The main targets of the UVF were Catholic civilians living in Northern Ireland. At the height of the Troubles, Catholics were consistently the victims of violence as their religion made them seem less loyal to

Britain, whose national religion was
Protestantism.

After identifying a further twelve suspects in
the Dublin and Monaghan bombings, all of
whom also had direct ties to the UVF, the
Irish police force sent its best detectives up
North to work with the Royal Ulster
Constabulary (RUC), the leading police force
in Northern Ireland at the time. Initially, the
RUC had been cooperating with Irish police,
but this all changed when they arrived in
Belfast.

After arriving in Belfast to question the
twenty people suspected to be involved with
the Dublin and Monaghan bombings, Irish
police were frustrated to find out that they
would not be allowed to question any of

their suspects. The RUC had jurisdiction and wanted to handle the investigations themselves. The Irish police were forced to leave, the only hope they had of solving the case now was left alongside their files with the RUC.

Ultimately, the Irish police's efforts were to be in vain. There is no record of any further communications between the Irish police or the RUC regarding the Dublin or Monaghan bombings. In their own final reports on the case, the RUC listed the suspects identified by the Irish police, but didn't specify whether any of the men were ever questioned or arrested. Three months after the bombings occurred, the case was officially filed as unsolved on both sides of the border.

Chapter 6

The Ulster Volunteer Force was far from being the only loyalist organizations fighting to maintain Northern Ireland's place within the United Kingdom. During the Troubles, the country was overrun with paramilitary groups who all had a mission of their own.

One of the most notorious loyalist groups in Northern Ireland was the Shankill Butcher gang, a paramilitary organization that got its name from the horrific murders it committed in the Shankill area of North Belfast. In the 1970's the gang was on a mission to show the Catholics living in Belfast just how unwelcome they truly were.

1972 was the deadliest year of the Troubles in Northern Ireland. In that year alone, nearly 500 people were killed. January saw Bloody Sunday, a horrific event that was permanently seared into the nation's memory, and July brought a series of bombings in the North by the Irish Republican Army, or IRA, an event that later became known as Bloody Friday.

As a way to protect their communities and gain a feeling of control amidst the madness, many citizens began joining the Ulster Volunteer Force, or UVF, and other similar paramilitary groups. Sparked by a nationwide fear of the IRA, these groups prepared for war. They were determined to protect themselves and their Protestant community against those whom they believed to be their enemies—Catholics and Republicans from the South.

The paramilitary underworld in Northern Ireland became rampant across the country, and before the nation could blink their eyes, these deadly groups had begun to take over.

On September 28, 1972, William Edward Pavis was shot dead outside of his home. Pavis was a Protestant civilian whom the UVF claimed had been selling weapons to the IRA. This was the ultimate betrayal to many Protestants living in the North. If Pavis had in fact been selling weapons to the IRA, he would have been helping the enemy defeat his own nation and those who shared his religion in the North.

Shortly after Pavis was shot, his murderer, a man by the name of Lenny Murphy was arrested and taken to Belfast's Crumlin Road prison. He was 20 years old at the time of the shooting. Alongside Murphy, Mervyn Connor was also arrested and sent to Crumlin Road. Connor had been Murphy's getaway driver and an accomplice to the crime.

Two months before Connor and Murphy's trial, Connor committed suicide by ingesting a large dose of cyanide. Next to his body was a written confession of the Pavis murder, which claimed Connor had acted alone and Murphy had participated in no way in the shooting. Police found this note suspicious as Connor had been working with them to cut a deal. Connor had agreed to testify against Murphy in exchange for an early release.

Despite investigators involved in the case believing that Murphy had been behind Connor's death and suicide note, Murphy was found guilty in court of only minor charges and served only two years in prison. The suicide note, which had been admitted into court as part of the defense's evidence, was largely responsible for Murphy dodging a murder charge. After his release in 1975, Murphy went on to mastermind one of the deadliest paramilitary groups Belfast ever saw — the Shankill Butchers.

Chapter 7

Lenny Murphy was a ruthless human being. He waged fear into those around him, and he used that fear to control and manipulate others into silence. By the time Murphy turned 23, he was thought to have already killed ten people.

People were drawn to Murphy, so it was no surprise that Murphy eventually gathered a crew to start his own gang. He set up his new gang's headquarters in the Shankill area, a loyalist working class neighborhood in Belfast. He initially recruited three henchmen to his operation, Sam McAllister, Robert Bates, and William Moore. These three men would be instrumental to the violence to come.

Like Lenny Murphy, McAllister, Bates, and Moore all shared a deep-seeded hatred of Catholics and backgrounds riddled with violence. McAllister was a 20-year-old young offender who had already won himself a reputation for violence; Moore was a meat packer who worked with butcher's knives and drove a black taxi; and Bates was a basher and petty criminal who had spent his entire childhood in and out of borstals.

Several other individuals joined and left the Butcher's gang over time, but Murphy, McAllister, Bates, and Moore were lifelong members. Murphy was undoubtedly the leader, using fear to keep the group in line and quiet about their actions. Murphy also had several connections in the UVF. While Murphy acknowledged that the Shankill Butchers and the UVF were working towards the same causes, both groups denied that they were working with each other, although it was widely believed that the Butchers were an outlet for the UVF to commit deadly acts without having to tarnish their official reputation.

Murphy flourished in his new role of gang leader, but being a major player in the underground loyalist movement wasn't enough for him. Murphy was determined to reach a level of sectarian savagery never before seen in Northern Ireland.

The first victim of the Shankill Butchers was Francis Crossen. Crossen's body was found by a Shankill resident on November 25, 1975 in plain sight strewn across a small alley off of Shankill road. Crossen had a deep wound in his throat that was still bleeding when police arrived on the scene. First responders to the scene noted that the wound was so deep they had initially thought Crossen had been completely decapitated.

Crossen had been a Catholic living in North Belfast. The father of two had been walking towards the city center just after midnight when four of the Butchers driving in Moore's black taxi spotted him.

The Butchers used the city's sectarian geography strategically in order to identify potential victims. They would patrol the Catholic areas of Belfast to find likely Catholic prey for their violence. Their mission was to send a message to all Catholics living in the area—you are not welcome.

When the Butchers saw Crossen walking alone through a Catholic neighborhood, they knew they had found a perfect target for their first major attack. They pulled Moore's taxi alongside Crossen and Murphy hit him with a wheel brace, rendering him unconscious. They then dragged the man into the taxi and drove to the alley where Crossen's body was found.

Crossen was taken out of the taxi and severely beaten by the men. When they were finished with him, Murphy brandished a butcher's knife and cut his victim's throat straight through to the spine. Crossen would be the first of many to die in this horrific way that became known as the Butcher's cutthroat killings.

The next victim of the Shankill Butchers was Edward McQuaid, who was shot from a moving black taxi while walking home from a party with his wife in January of 1976. The couple was seen leaving a popular drinking spot for Catholics by the Butchers, who followed them down the road. When the timing was right, the black taxi pulled alongside the couple and shot McQuaid in the head. McQuaid's wife ran to the nearest house and called police, but by the time they arrived the black taxi was long gone.

After McQuaid's death, the Belfast police began to worry they had an epidemic on their hands. There were several connections between McQuaid and Crossen's deaths even though they had been killed in very different ways. In both cases, the victims had been Catholic men walking in Catholic neighborhoods in the sectarian areas of North Belfast. In fact, the two were killed less than a mile away from each other. In addition, both McQuaid's wife and witnesses to Crossen's death had identified a black taxi as being the vehicle involved in the killings.

When Thomas Quinn was found dead in a Shankill Alley with his throat cut through to the spine less than a month after McQuaid was shot, police were certain all three deaths were connected.

After Quinn's death, police knew they were looking for multiple people working together. Both Quinn and Crossen were large men so it would've taken more than one person to overpower, abduct, beat, and kill the men. As well, police knew they were looking for a loyalist group due to the geographic patterns of the killings, and the fact that all three victims had been Catholics. They began to fear they were dealing with a paramilitary group gone rogue.

Investigators to this day maintain that at the time of these deaths they had no idea who was responsible. They had been diligently investigating the crimes but had no major leads. Many living in Belfast at the time found that hard to believe — the whole city had been paralyzed in fear by the Shankill

Butchers who made their presence known in the community.

Many loyalist leaders in the area also allegedly knew exactly who had been behind the cutthroat killings, but were too paralyzed by their fear to talk to the police. Murphy incited fear into many people, especially those who could potentially get in his way. This is best illustrated by the fact that the Shankill Butchers were initially part of the UVF, but had gone renegade when they started their campaign of murder.

The UVF was questioned about the killings by police, but they said nothing about Murphy or his gang. They were too frightened to cross the man who was capable of such horrific acts.

Only two weeks after Thomas Quinn was found dead, the Shankill Butchers claimed their third cutthroat victim. The man was Francis Rice, a Catholic civilian. He was found with his throat slashed in the usual style in a side street entryway off of Shankill Road. Police still had no prime suspects in the string of murders. The Butchers were winning.

One aspect of the cutthroat killings that made it difficult for police to track down those responsible was the random nature of each of the killings. Besides the fact that all the victims were Catholics, or were spotted in Catholic neighborhoods, they were being targeted randomly. None of the victims had any connections to each other or their killers.

People seemed to be getting plucked off the street for no good reason.

But the Shankill Butchers believed they were doing good work. After Murphy was imprisoned, psychologists labelled him as a functioning psychopath. He had an extreme hatred of Catholics, and his lack of remorse for his shocking crimes suggested that he viewed his victims more like animals than humans. Their lives were worth less because of their religion, they deserved to die.

Part of what allowed Murphy and his gang to think this way about Catholics was the fact that they had an ardent military mindset. They were committed to their cause, and they truly felt that they were protecting their homes and neighborhoods.

They were at war; the regular rules of life no longer applied.

The people of Belfast could feel the terror of the Shankill Butchers in the air — the terror the Butchers brought made them legends in their own time. People in North Belfast, especially Catholics, stopped going out at night. People felt restricted to their homes after the sun went down. For the few brave who still ventured out from their homes after dark, their worst nightmare became being approached by a black taxi.

Understandably, the 1970's was a time of great terror for Catholics living in Northern Ireland, and those living in North Belfast began to get fed up with the local police. By the late 1970's, Catholics were still being shot at in the street by the Shankill Butchers and the police still had no one in custody and no prime suspects. The Catholic community felt abandoned, many believed that the police were simply turning a blind eye to the crimes.

Amazingly, in March of 1976, Lenny Murphy made a shocking error that quickly leads to his arrest, turning the public opinion of police around just in time. On a March evening, two women were driving down Cliftonville Rd when they were shot at by a passing vehicle. The crime was not initially thought to be at the hands of the Butchers as the vehicle holding the gunman was not the classic black taxi of legend.

The gunman abandoned his vehicle in a loyalist neighborhood and set it on fire, drawing police to the scene. When they arrived, they identified the vehicle as being the gunman's and noticed something odd — the gun had been abandoned just up the road from the burning car. On a hunch, police believed that the gun may have been left as an accident so they didn't disturb it. They did however put the area on surveillance.

Incredibly, after dark the next day the gunman returned to collect his weapon and was promptly arrested. It was then that police discovered their mystery gunman was none other than Lenny Murphy himself. Murphy was jailed for possession of a firearm with intention to cause harm, although the police suspected he was guilty of much more.

Chapter 8

In August of 1976, Lenny Murphy, leader of the Shankill Butchers gang that was terrorizing Catholics in North Belfast, was safely tucked away in jail. This would be the end to the wave of terror across the city, or so investigators thought.

On August 2, 1976, Corneilus Neeson was found beaten to death at the junction of Manor Street and Cliftonville road, dead-smack in the middle of the Shankill Butchers' hunting grounds. Neeson had been walking through his Catholic neighborhood when he was apparently abducted. When he was found, he had had his throat slashed with a hatchet.

History repeated itself again on October 30, 1976 when Stephen McCann, a 20-year-old Catholic civilian was found with his throat slashed near a Catholic community center. It was clear that Murphy was able to still command his men while behind bars.

Two months later, Joseph Morrissey, a 52-year-old Catholic civilian was found in the same place as McCann. He had been murdered in the exact same manner.

The Shankill Butchers would claim one more cutthroat victim before making another fatal error, one that lead to their eventual capture by chance.

On March 30, 1977, Francis Cassidy became the last Catholic to have his throat slashed by the Butchers. He had been walking home from the pub the night he was abducted by the gang. His body was discovered in the morning in the Highfern Gardens. Only a couple weeks after Cassidy's body was found, the Shankill Butchers were back out on the hunt. This time, however, things did not go quite to plan.

Gerard McLaverty was walking home from his friend's house around 11:30pm on May 10, 1977 when he was picked up by the Shankill Butchers. He was abducted and taken to an abandoned doctor's office on Shankill road where he was beaten and tortured for several hours with a meat cleaver and fire iron among other instruments.

The Butcher's plan for McLaverty went well beyond torture though. After hours of inflicting pain on the man, the Butchers cut McLaverty's wrists and partially strangled him with wire. When the man fell unconscious, they left him in the entryway of the abandoned doctor's office to die.

Miraculously, McLaverty awoke from his unconscious state and was able to find help before he bled to death. He was hospitalized for his injuries for over a week. The terrible cuts along his arms left disfiguring scars for the rest of his life. When he was released from hospital, McLaverty retraced his journey on the night of his adduction alongside investigators in an effort to try and help them find the men that almost took his life.

While retracing the journey that almost led to his death, McLaverty made a shocking discovery. While driving down Shankill road, McLaverty spotted a group of men walking down the road together, and he recognized the one in the middle. It was Sam McAllister, one of the men who had spent hours torturing him just a week earlier.

Walking with Sam McAllister was also Benjamin Edwards, a second man who had been involved in McLaverty's abduction. He did not recognize the third man, but was able to describe William Moore and his black taxi. Later, investigators were able to match fibers from McLaverty's clothing to fibers found in Moore's vehicle.

After this forensic evidence was discovered, Moore was immediately taken into custody alongside his companions. Moore was a person of special interest to police as he was the owner of the mythical black taxi that spread fear into the hearts of Catholics, and that had been involved in almost all of the Butchers' attacks.

In the face of the fiber evidence, Moore confessed to kidnapping McLaverty but refused to name any of the men he worked with. He also denied any involvement in the cutthroat murders or any of the shootings police had linked to the gang.

While interrogating Moore, police noticed something interesting about the man; he was completely stricken by fear of the man he worked for — Lenny Murphy. Investigators used this knowledge to their advantage. In order to get a confession from Moore, they lied and told him they had further evidence that linked him to all the cutthroat murders. If he was unable to provide any evidence in his defense, he would be charged with the murders and likely put away for life.

Moore was terrified, but not ready to talk. He did however insist that he was innocent, saying he knew who had committed the murders although he wouldn't say who. This was all investigators needed for their plan.

After Moore admitted to knowing more information about the murders, they placed him back in his cell with the final thought that Moore had already ratted out Murphy with this minor confession. If he was able to provide the police with more information about the murders they could protect him, but if he wasn't able to, they couldn't be certain Moore was in trouble. They would not intervene, and Moore would be left alone to deal with Murphy and the other Butchers alone. And the word on the street was that the Butchers didn't take kindly towards snitches.

After only a few hours, Moore was ready to talk. He was re-interrogated by police and admitted his full involvement in the cutthroat killings. He stated that Murphy had committed the first three murders before being imprisoned at which point he took over on Murphy's orders. He was terrified by the man and followed all of his orders in fear of his own personal safety.

When Lenny Murphy was confronted by Moore's confession, he simply laughed it off.

After Moore's confession, Belfast police were able to identify and arrest eleven other members of the Shankill Butchers, eight of whom eventually confessed to the cutthroat murders as well as the killing of eleven other people. It was a great victory for police, who had yet to connect the eleven murders to the Butchers.

The Butchers had shot five Catholic men aged 45-59 at a bar on the same night; they had also murdered two Protestant truck drivers they thought were Catholics due to their location; three men were killed during loyalist feuding; and worst of all, they had murdered a 10-year-old boy when they bombed an Easter parade.

With nineteen murders between them, they were, at the time, the most prolific serial killers in British history.

Chapter 9

The Shankill Butchers went on trial in February of 1979. Eleven of the men were all tried together in front of a packed courtroom. Although there was no doubt in anyone's mind that Murphy had been involved in the crimes committed during his imprisonment, he was not part of the trial. Many of the Butchers who confessed refused to name Murphy out of fear.

All eleven men who went on trial pleaded guilty to the crimes they committed. The gang was sentenced to a cumulative 2000 years in prison, a number many Catholics who had been living in fear for years found satisfying. It gave them hope for their futures in Belfast for the first time in years.

Three years after the Shankill Butchers stood on trial, Lenny Murphy was released from prison. He was quickly backed on police radar when he became the primary suspect in a series of murders that had begun immediately after his release. It seemed that the head Butcher had not lost his taste for blood while he was behind bars, and he had some debts that needed repaying. Murphy was back on the rampage, leaving only death in his wake. He needed to be stopped; it was only a matter of who would be the one to do the job.

Three months after Murphy was released from jail, Murphy was ratted on by members of his new company, who had already tired of being under his fearful thumb. These members of Murphy's company gave the

IRA, the Irish Republican Army, intelligence regarding Murphy's movements around Belfast. Murphy was shot by the IRA in Glencairn, an area that was used to dispose of many of his own victims. It was seen as poetic justice by most.

While the Shankill Butchers' actions were condemned by the UVF and most other loyalist forces in Northern Ireland at the time, there are still some in Belfast who glorify the Shankill Butchers and the lives they took on behalf of their country. Murphy was honored as a military hero after his death, and his headstone was marked with the words Here lies a soldier. William Moore was awarded the same honor when he died in 2009.

Many have used the Troubles as a way to justify the Shankill Butchers' actions, excusing their murders is heroic actions instead of the unnecessary taking of lives they truly were. Nine of the nineteen total victims of the Shankill Butchers had been Protestant in the end. The Troubles simply gave Murphy an excuse to serially kill without consequence.

Not a single member of the Shankill Butchers served the entirety of their prison sentences. All of the convicted Shankill Butchers have been released from jail, and as of 2013, nine of the eleven convicted were still alive and well, living in Northern Ireland.

Chapter 10

Though history has not been kind to the Irish people, their divided nation helped form a unique — if fractured — cultural identity. More importantly, they have begun to heal. As with all wars, the Irish revolutionary conflict took many lives in many horrific ways. It also featured scores of atrocities undertaken by evildoers masquerading as nationalists and protectors.

Not all monsters have the benefit of a war to distance them from their crimes. Most are ordinary people. Counted among Ireland's otherwise cheerful public are some of the world's most heinous killers. Though their motives vary, one thing remains the same —

they valued their vicious goals more than they valued human life.

In March 2005, a dismembered corpse was pulled from Dublin's Royal Canal. It was a gruesome scene — a headless torso with its arms and legs hacked off. Without a head, it was a long and almost impossible task for the Irish police to identify the victim, let alone investigate who was responsible for the horrific crime. The police thought it was a ritual killing, but soon the story took an even more cynical turn. Five months later, Linda and Charlotte Mulhall were arrested. Later, they would be dubbed the scissor sisters.

Linda and Charlotte Mulhall grew up in a small estate in southwest Dublin along with their four siblings, their grandfather, and their mother, Kathleen. As they got older, both girls had their own demons and troubles. By the age of twenty-five, Linda had four children from a previous relationship with an ex-high school sweetheart. In the year 2000, she began a new relationship that was plagued with violence and abuse.

Linda Mulhall was the older of the two sisters; she was in her early thirties at the time of the killing. She was unemployed, had a history of alcohol and heroin abuse, and was dating a sadist who beat her children. Linda knew about the abuse long before she reported it to police. Because of this, her children were removed from her care after she did report the beatings. In an attempt to regain guardianship of her children, Linda had tried to clean up her act. She stopped using heroin, reduced her alcohol consumption, and moved back in with her mother for support.

While Linda Mulhall was no shining daughter, her younger sister Charlotte was no better. Charlotte was described as being the drifter of the family. She spent her time between her mother's home and various other addresses across the Dublin area. She would stay on her friend's couches, or with her boyfriend of the week, but she never had a place to herself to call home. Charlotte had never worked a day in her life when she helped her mother and sister kill the man found in the Royal Canal the day before her twenty-second birthday.

As well as drifting through addresses across Dublin, Charlotte also drifted in and out of jail. She had no major offences to her name, but had accumulated several nights in the local jail for petty crimes. To make pocket cash, Charlotte worked the streets as a prostitute alongside her mother, Kathleen, who allegedly introduced her to the work.

In 2002, the Mulhall family was turned upside down when Kathleen made the impulse decision to leave her husband, John, for the African immigrant Farah Swaleh Noor, whom she had met in a nightclub the previous year. John and Kathleen had been married for twenty-nine years. Noor immediately moved into the family's home before the couple decided to start fresh together in Cork just months later.

The new couple stayed in Cork for a couple of years, along the way Noor picked up and lost a variety of part time jobs, but nothing ever lasted. There was a lot of alcohol drank in this time, and a fair amount of drug use, but all-in-all they pair kept their noses clean and out of trouble.

When Noor continued to lose job after job in Cork, the couple decided to try their luck again in Dublin. They lived in various hostels and bed and breakfast accommodations around the city center before finally settling down in the Richmond Cottages complex just outside of Dublin. Noor was becoming well-known in Dublin for his abusive behaviors, but what his friends and new girlfriend didn't know was

that he had an even darker past, one he had
managed to keep secret.

When Noor first came to Ireland, he claimed
he was a Somalian refugee. He had been run
out of his country, he had seen his wife being
killed in the streets, and he had no idea
where his family was. Kathleen bought the
story hook, line, and sinker. In reality, Noor
was from Kenya, and he had a wife and
three children there.

While living in Kenya, Noor had heard
stories of Ireland, but not the same ones that
generally draw tourists to the country of
rolling hills. Noor was once told that Ireland
provided asylum to refugees, and that the
Irish government gave these refugees money

for doing nothing. It seemed like too sweet a deal for the man to pass up.

Noor arrived in Ireland in December of 1996. When he arrived at customs he had no passport or ID. He told the men working there that he had fled from Somalia so quickly that he had had no time to collect any documents. Amazingly, he was granted entry into the country and began collecting refugee welfare from the state.

Noor quickly made a name for himself amongst those who frequented the same bars as him around Dublin. When he was sober, he was a great friend. He got along with everyone. But once he had had a drink too many he became a violent individual. The Dublin police also became very familiar with

Noor. He was detained several times a month for getting in bar brawls, and had been accused of rape by multiple women.

Linda, Charlotte, and Kathleen's abuse of alcohol and drugs mixed with Noor's violent nature would result in one of the most grotesque murders in Irish history.

Chapter 11

On Sunday March 20, 2005, Charlotte and
Linda Mulhall were living together in
Dublin. Linda had just regained custody of
her children and she wanted to spend the
day with her 11-year-old son. Charlotte,
though, had different plans. She was turning
twenty-two the next day and she wanted to
start her birthday celebrations early.

At 11am that Sunday morning, Charlotte,
eager to start celebrating her upcoming
birthday, brought out a large bottle of vodka.
After some pestering, she convinced her
sister to have a drink with her. Linda was
initially hesitant, as she had her son with her
that day, but eventually she agreed. That

drink would become the first of many for the pair that fateful Sunday.

A short time later, Kathleen called Charlotte and invited both her and her sister to join her in the city alongside her boyfriend Farah Swaleh Noor. Charlotte jumped at the chance for a bigger celebration, but Linda remained unconvinced. The sisters had different opinions of Kathleen's boyfriend Noor. Linda was more affected by her parent's failed relationship that ended with Noor entering the picture. She never forgave Noor for being the man that broke up her parents.

Charlotte on the other hand was young and pragmatic. She accepted Noor into the family simply because her mom loved him.

Eventually, Linda conceded to her younger sister and agreed to join her and their mother for a day of drinking. The pair spent the next hour getting ready, they had a few more drinks while trying out different outfits and applying their makeup. Their dramatic looks would be etched into the minds of the public for years to come.

The two girls had very distinctive looks. They both appeared in court everyday wearing distinctly heavy makeup. Linda was more feminine — she sported long, blonde hair whereas Charlotte preferred to keep her dark locks braided back tight to her scalp. These overly dramatic styles worked against Linda and Charlotte though, with many believing it was the main reason they became known as the scissor sisters — a suggestively violent name for two violent girls.

At around 1:15pm, Linda and Charlotte caught a bus into the Dublin city center and met up with Kathleen and Noor. Kathleen and Noor had also been drinking all morning, and they showed signs of it. They were on a three-day bender, and were still in the mood for more. It was three days after St Patrick's day, and both Noor and Kathleen had been drinking solidly since then.

Sunday may have started as a somewhat normal day of drinking for the Mulhalls and Farah Swaleh Noor, but it was about to take a serious turn for the worse—a horrifying turn that would inexplicably change their lives forever.

At around 2pm, Charlotte, Linda, Kathleen, and Farah Swaleh Noor headed for the boardwalk along the River Liffey. As all four were on welfare, they couldn't afford to go to the pub for the afternoon so Noor bought a bottle of vodka and four bottles of Coke. Everyone was in good spirits and Kathleen and Noor were getting along well.

To liven up the party, Linda brought out a bag of Ecstasy she had. She took one pill herself and gave another to Charlotte. After some persuasion, their mother Kathleen decided to join in and also took a tablet of the hallucinogenic drug. Noor wasn't offered any of the drugs, as Linda and Charlotte were aware of his violent tendencies, and they didn't want anything to ruin their day.

Over the course of three hours, Linda, Charlotte and Kathleen all took two more pills of ecstasy each. They were having a good time, but Noor was getting progressively drunk and he began to pick fights and get aggressive with Kathleen. With the mood taking a turn for the worse, the four decided to return back to Kathleen and Noor's home in the Richmond Cottages estate, just outside of the city.

Kathleen's house was only a ten or fifteen minute walk away, but it would prove to be one of the most eventful walks of their lives. When the four companions reached O'Connell Street, Noor spotted a young Chinese boy across the street. The boy had been about five or six. Noor became very emotional at the sight of the boy and began to attempt to hug the child. He started crying and yelling that this was his own son. When the young boy became upset, Kathleen yelled at Noor until he stopped. They then continued to fight and argue for the remainder of the journey. Linda started to fight with Kathleen and Noor as well, after their own feuding began to annoy them.

By the time the foursome reached Kathleen's house, they were all back on better terms. Charlotte had managed to calm Linda down, and they were ready to get back to partying. This new peace didn't last for long though. At the house, Kathleen spiked Noor's beer with one of Linda's ecstasy tablets, which Kathleen crushed up and mixed into the drink. This sent Noor's aggressive behaviors over the edge.

Noor sat next to Linda on the couch and began to put his arm around her. When she protested, he started whispering sexual innuendos in her ear. Linda was a beautiful girl, and Noor seemed to only have eyes for her that night.

When Linda moved to get off the couch, Noor forced her back. Linda began shouting for help, grabbing the attention of Charlotte and Kathleen who then joined her in berating the man. Noor, who had been convicted of rape in the past, and accused of many more, wasn't prepared to take Linda's no for an answer, and a fight broke out.

 After much struggle, Charlotte was able to prise Noor's grip off of her sister, but Noor immediately began attacking Kathleen. He started pushing and dragging her towards the bedroom, all the while making slicing gestures with his fingers along his throat. The three women took this gesture as a serious threat. They believed it meant Noor was going to cut Kathleen's throat.

In a panic, Kathleen began pleading for her daughters to kill the man who was dragging her to her death. She yelled to Linda and Charlotte that if they didn't kill Farah Swaleh Noor now, she herself would be dead soon. She was terrified of the man she called her lover.

Drunk, high, and full of adrenaline, Charlotte grabbed a utility knife and jabbed it into Noor's throat from behind, leaving a four inch slice along his neck. From this point onwards, there was no going back for the women. They would have finished what Charlotte had started that fateful evening.

Noor fell to the floor, but was still alive, so Charlotte jumped on him and slit his throat a second time. When this also failed to kill the man, Linda grabbed a hammer and smashed it into Noor's head again, and again, and again. Linda was unable to recall later how many times she struck Noor with the hammer; she just knew she did it with all her might. Together, Charlotte and Linda launched a brutal attack on the man who was surely dead by then.

While Linda and Charlotte were busy

beating her boyfriend to death, Kathleen sat in the living room and watched television, ignoring the plethora of sounds coming from her bedroom where

Her lover now lay dead.

When Linda and Charlotte ended their frenzied attack on Farah Swaleh Noor, the harsh reality of what they just committed began to sink in. Charlotte alone had stabbed the man over 22 times, and Linda had beaten him relentlessly. It was a horrific scene. In shock, the two girls went out to their mother and told them what had happened. Kathleen's response—get his body out of my house.

The three women knew they would have a difficult time disposing of Noor's body — the man had been much larger than any of them. They decided the easiest way would be to cut up his body, so they dragged Noor's corpse to their mother's small bathroom and began the dismemberment.

Armed with just a utility knife, a bread knife, and a hammer, Linda and Charlotte began sawing off Noor's arms, legs, penis, and head. Charlotte started sawing Noor's Right leg above the knee while Linda took the hammer to his shin. They also used the hammer to break through the leg bones. The sisters repeated this process for the remaining limbs, tossing the eight separate pieces into the shower behind them. The whole process took the sisters over four hours.

After chopping up their mother's boyfriend, Charlotte and Linda Mulhall were faced with the dilemma of how to get rid of the pieces. They decided to wrap each body part in a black plastic bag, and placed them into three duffel bags. They then began to clean the apartment so thoroughly that it took investigators over three examinations of the scene to confirm that the murder had in fact taken place there.

At around 7:00am the next morning, Charlotte, Linda, and Kathleen set about disposing of Noor's body parts. They carried the duffel bags through the morning commute traffic to the Ballybeg Bridge, which provided a crossing over the Royal Canal. The three women began throwing the individually wrapped body parts into the water, except for the head and the penis. It was a birthday Charlotte would never forget.

The three women now needed to get rid of Noor's head, so they loaded it and the murder weapons into a backpack and caught the bus to Tymon Park in Tallaght. The whereabouts of Noor's dismembered penis still remains a mystery.

In Tymon Park, Charlotte used the utility knife she had stabbed Noor with to dig a hole under a park bench. They buried the head and threw the murder weapons into the nearby lake. They had finally wiped their hands clean of all traces of the grisly deed they had committed the day before. They then swore to each other that they would never tell anyone what they had done.

Chapter 12

Farah Swaleh Noor's dismembered body parts were discovered in the Royal Canal on March 30, 2005. News of the discovery, and the subsequent manhunt by the Dublin police, was splashed across every media outlet possible. It frightened the girls, and Linda decided she needed to take more precautions with Noor's head.

Linda dug up Noor's head from its grave in Tymon Park, took it to a nearby isolated field, and smashed it to smithereens while drinking a bottle of vodka. She could finally let it rest.

The Dublin police were initially baffled by the dismembered body they had found in the Royal Canal. Without the head, they were having a hard time identifying the victim. Initially the police thought the victim was a white male because the pigmentation in Noor's skin was degraded after being in the water for so long. It wasn't until the coroner assigned to the case removed the remaining clothing that they saw their victim was actually black.

 It took investigators 100 days and help from the public in order to finally identify the remains as belonging to Farah Swaleh Noor. When they were clearly getting nowhere with the case, Dublin police decided to publish photos of the shirt that was found on the dismembered torso. Luckily for police, a Somali man recognized the distinctive jersey as being the shirt he last saw his friend Farah

Swaleh Noor wearing, and when he thought about it, he hadn't seen or heard from Noor since mid-March, the time around when the dismembered remains were found. Putting two and two together, the man immediately contacted police.

Once police had conclusively identified the remains as Farah Swaleh Noor, the case was blown wide open. Police began questioning Noor's last-known girlfriend Kathleen Mulhall, and when they got a bad feeling about her answers, they contacted her two sons who were in prison for driving offences.

Amazingly, over the course of several prison visits, Kathleen had confided in her sons about the murder, breaking her pact with Charlotte and Linda. Kathleen's two sons willingly gave information about the murder to police in exchange for early releases.

When it became known to the public that Charlotte and Linda Mulhall were behind the murders, they became overnight sensations. Now publicly dubbed the scissor sisters, Charlotte was found guilty of murder and Linda was found guilty of manslaughter in court a year and a half after they committed one of the most odd and macabre murders Ireland had ever seen.

Chapter 13

After the murder and dismemberment of Farah Swaleh Noor at the hands of Charlotte and Linda Mulhall, Dublin citizens were positive that no crime more bizarre could ever be committed in their city. When Graham Dwyer murdered Elaine O'Hara in 2012, he was out to prove them wrong.

Elaine O'Hara was reported missing in August 2012 by her father, Frank O'Hara. He feared the worst as he normally spoke to her each day, but hadn't been able to get in contact with her for nearly two days.

Initially, police and O'Hara's family and friends feared she had committed suicide due a significant history of mental health problems. O'Hara was easily stressed, and when she was confronted with pressure she would often end up in the hospital. She also had a history of self-harming. Co-workers of O'Hara would often see her covered in scratches and cuts, something that O'Hara never tried to hide.

O'Hara's problems with mental health began in her mid-teens. She became withdrawn after being bullied and losing one of her good friends to a car accident. She attempted suicide for the first time at sixteen-years-old. O'Hara had locked herself in the bathroom and slashed her wrists. After her mother noticed she had been gone for a while, she forced the door open only to see her own daughter sitting in the bathtub, bleeding out. Since then, O'Hara's family were very involved in her life, they were her main support system. Her parents got her help right away as soon as she needed it, and O'Hara had always been very good at letting them know exactly when she needed help.

As an adult, O'Hara found solace tutoring young children. It was her passion and gave her the light she needed to continue working through her problems with depression and anxiety. She found it easier to relate to the children she worked with than other adults. In 2001, O'Hara landed her dream job. She was hired as a childcare assistant in the same elementary school her mother worked at. This connection brought the already close pair even closer.

Sadly, O'Hara's mother died six months later after being diagnosed with cancer. It was a shock to O'Hara, whose mother had been her guardian angel for years. It was clear to everyone around O'Hara that she was having a tough time dealing with her mother's death. Especially to her father Frank, who O'Hara had begun to go to for emotional support.

O'Hara was losing to her father, and she spoke to him every day. In an effort to help her feel more independent, Frank helped O'Hara purchase an apartment to live. O'Hara had trouble with money and was facing the possibility of moving back in with her father. Together they fixed up the apartment to make it somewhere O'Hara could relax, feel at peace, and be happy.

Despite her father's help, O'Hara's troubles began to become too much for her to manage. In July 2012, O'Hara checked into a psychiatric hospital. Three weeks later, O'Hara completed her treatment. She was very excited to leave the hospital. She was reunited with her father, and had volunteered to be a tourist guide in the upcoming tall ships festival in Dublin. She was even joking to friends on the phone about meeting a handsome sailor at the festival who would sweep her off her feet and sail her away from all her troubles. She was in the best spirits she had been in since her mother died.

O'Hara had been released from the psychiatric hospital around noon on August 22, 2012. Shortly after leaving the hospital,

O'Hara and her father, who had picked her up, visited O'Hara's mother's grave at the Shanganagh Cemetery. The next day, Frank hears O'Hara was a no-show at the festival. Worried, he tried to call her phone, but got no answer. He also paid a visit to O'Hara's apartment, which he had the key to. When he entered the apartment, he found no sign of O'Hara anywhere except for her phone sitting on her bedside table. He knew something was wrong.

The next day, there was still no word of O'Hara so Frank returned to her apartment with a friend. Nothing had changed since the day before, it was clear that O'Hara had not returned over the night. On this second visit, Frank also noticed O'Hara's purse sitting in her living room, an item she seldom left the house without. This also meant that wherever O'Hara was, she had no money or ID on her.

Frank began scrambling to find his daughter. He checked with the hospital O'Hara had just checked out of to see if she had returned. She wasn't there. In a bid to retrace O'Hara's steps the day before she failed to show up to the tall ships festival, Frank went to his wife's grave at the Shanganagh Cemetery where he made startling discovery. O'Hara's car was in the cemetery's parking lot. Inside, Frank found cigarettes, a lighter, and a charger for a Nokia phone—a different kind of phone than O'Hara's.

After discovering O'Hara's car so near her mother's grave, Frank immediately began to fear that O'Hara had taken her own life. The cemetery was near the ocean. O'Hara could have easily parked her car, said goodbye to her mother, and then crossed the street to the beach and presumably drowned herself in the dark waves. Frank drove straight from the cemetery to the police station where he reported her missing.

Local police immediately classified O'Hara as a missing person, and began a localized search of the area with the public's help. All eyes were looking out for O'Hara. In their search, police first looked at security footage taken outside of O'Hara's apartment building. They were able to see that she had arrived home the day her father picked her up from the hospital and had again left her apartment about an hour and a half later wearing a dark sweatshirt and sweatpants. She had told her father that she was going to stay in and get some rest before helping out with the festival the next day. No one had any idea that she had gone back out that night.

In the security footage, police also noticed O'Hara using a cell phone that was different than the one her father found in her apartment. This phone was different than the iPhone she used to message with her father and friends. It was a brand of phone that no one knew she owned, and presumably was a different number than the one her friends and family had.

A week after O'Hara's disappearance, police returned to the area O'Hara's car was found in. Not only did the parking lot border on her mother's cemetery, it also bordered a large forested park. Police canvassed the park area and asked those around if they had seen O'Hara the previous week. One man recalled seeing O'Hara after being shown her picture. He had briefly spoken to her the day she disappeared. O'Hara had been walking alone down the path he was jogging on and had asked him if he knew where a railway bridge was nearby. When he said he didn't, O'Hara kept walking and the jogger continued on his way.

The man who had run into O'Hara in the forest that night was at the time the last known person to see O'Hara alive. He had described her as being pre-occupied, distracted. She seemed like she was in distress. Because of this, and the lack of any other evidence of her being in the area, police began to theorize that O'Hara must have simply continued down the trail until she hit the ocean, where she kept walking until she drowned.

O'Hara's friends and family began to accept the police's theory, although it was hard for many of them at first. When she left the hospital, O'Hara seemed happier than she had been for years. They found it hard to understand why she decided to take her own life when she finally seemed to be healing for the first time.

Chapter 14

For the next thirteen months, O'Hara remained classified as a missing person. It wasn't until September 2013 that this would change. At a reservoir 25 km away from where O'Hara had last been seen, three old friends got together for a chat. While they were chatting on a bridge, they noticed a yellow rope floating in the water with something shiny attached to the end. It had been a dry summer and the reservoir was low. They managed to fish out the rope and attached objects. What they found was completely shocking.

Attached to the yellow rope floating in the reservoir was a dark blue sweater and a pair of handcuffs. Intrigued by this find, the men continued to fish out more objects from the body of water. They found more bondage gear, including a mask with a ball gag and several more pairs of handcuffs. They also found a backpack with more bondage paraphernalia and clothing inside.

After discovering the horde of bondage gear and clothing, the men had a bit of a laugh and left the items on the side of the road. They were unusual items to find, and the men thought that someone must have dumped them out of embarrassment or anger. One of the men, however, had a bad feeling about how the items came to the reservoir. He returned the next day to collect the items and brought them to the local police station where they were examined.

The police officer in charge of examining the items found in the reservoir, Officer O'Donoghue, also had a bad feeling about how the items came to be dumped in the water. From the beginning, O'Donoghue treated the items as evidence of a crime and stored them carefully. He also returned to the reservoir on a number of occasions to see if he could find more connected items. He was able to retrieve two cellphones and a set of keys that were traced to Elaine O'Hara from the loyalty card tags that were attached. This set of keys was the first sign of O'Hara in thirteen months.

Two days after Officer O'Donoghue found O'Hara's keys in the reservoir, O'Hara's skeletal remains were found two miles away by a young lady out walking her dog. She had noticed a pair of sweatpants that look highly degraded. When she nudged them with her foot, she noticed there was still a shoe tucked inside of them. Her dog ran off, but when he returned to her side, he was carrying a large bone in his mouth. It was clear that these were not the remains of an animal, but the remains of a human. The young woman immediately called police.

After investigators arrived on scene, they began to collect the remains. This was made difficult by the fact that animals in the area had scattered the body pieces around the local area. They were only able to recover two thirds of the remains. The body's skull and hand bones were never found; however, the jaw bone was still intact, enabling investigators to match the remaining teeth to

Elaine O'Hara's dental records. It was the second major coincidental break in the case of O'Hara's disappearance within 48-hours.

O'Hara's family had just begun to accept that she had killed herself when police visited them with the news that O'Hara's remains had been found. At this point, police also told O'Hara's father that they suspected she had been murdered. There was no evidence of suicide at the scene or on O'Hara's remains. It was a complete shock.

News of O'Hara's murder sent a frenzy of fear around the Dublin area. A killer had been walking amongst them completely undetected for more than a year. The police were under a lot of pressure to solve the case without having to rely on more coincidences to dredge up more evidence. They had to take action, and O'Hara's murder became their top priority.

Investigators began to examine the cellphones O'Donoghue found in the reservoir and found that one was noticeably similar to the one seen with O'Hara on the security footage from the night she disappeared. Amazingly, they were able to turn on one of the cellphones and read the text messages that had been sent to the phone during the months before her disappearance. These text messages told a horrifying tale of manipulation, domination, and violence.

It was easy for investigators to identify which cellphone had been O'Hara's and which had been her killers. One phone had saved the other's number as MSTR, for master, another clue that connected the murder with BDSM and bondage. Through the series of text messages police began to discover that O'Hara had been in a sexual relationship with someone, someone who dreamed of stabbing women while he had sex with them, and someone who liked to control O'Hara. The other phone had her number saved in it as SLV, for slave.

Police realized that they needed to find a way to identify the owner of the cellphone belonging to the master. Unfortunately, the phone was a burner phone. It was a prepaid phone that only texted one number — O'Hara's. Investigators decided to examine CCTV footage of O'Hara's apartment to see if they could identify any men who regularly visited her home.

Investigators watched months of this CCTV footage, and eventually a pattern began to emerge. They were able to isolate one particular man who visited O'Hara quite regularly. One week before O'Hara's disappearance, he was spotted leaving O'Hara's apartment building with a backpack that looked similar to the one found stuffed full with bondage gear in the reservoir.

O'Hara's apartment was examined once again. An analysis of O'Hara's computer and wardrobe confirmed that she had been heavily involved in the word of bondage and BDSM.

O'Hara had an active profile on the adult fetish website Alt.com. It was through this website that she met Graham Dwyer; a young, attractive architect who had been online looking for someone to help him control his sex-driven urges to rape, stab, or kill.

O'Hara and Dwyer's profiles and sexual desires were complimentary—Dwyer wanted to control, overpower, inflict pain, and O'Hara was willing to do almost anything it took to feel desired. The two began an intense sexual relationship. Investigators later found violent sex tapes and fragments of graphic emails on O'Hara's laptop. Their relationship had been most prominent in 2008 but had fizzled out when O'Hara began to seek help for her mental health problems. It had rekindled in March 2011.

Although Dwyer's sexual interests were violent, there was very little in his background to suggest that he would be the perpetrator of violence. Dwyer was born on September 13, 1972 in County Cork. He had three siblings, two brothers and a sister. Dwyer had been an intellectual child and had always succeeded in school. After completing secondary school he moved to Dublin to study architecture. It had been a lifelong dream of his.

Soon after moving to Dublin, Dwyer met Emer McShae, his first ever girlfriend. The two seemed happy in their love for one another, and less than a year since the two became a couple, McShae became pregnant with a son. The two wouldn't stay together for long though. By McShae's account, the longer the two went out, the more honest and aggressive Dwyer became about sexual fantasies they had. She admitted that Dwyer often told her he fantasized about stabbing a woman during sex, and he began to bring a kitchen knife into their bedroom. McShae left Dwyer after he became overly aggressive with her and began to pretend to stab her during sex. Each time she asked him to stop; he pressed the knife into her skin a bit harder.

Only a year after McShae ended their relationship, Dwyer had found another romantic interest. In 1997, Dwyer began dating Gemma Healy. It was also around this time that Dwyer began to search the internet and local classified ads for others into fetish fantasies instead of performing them with Healy. Healy and Dwyer married five years later. Healy later stated she was unaware that Dwyer had been unfaithful to her for the majority of their relationship. To those in the dark about his sexual fantasies, Dwyer was just an average hard-working man supporting his wife and now three children.

Any picture of innocence Irish police had for Dwyer was quickly erased the more they delved into the text messages recovered from the cellphones from the reservoir. Thousands of text messages passed between Dwyer and O'Hara. The texts from Dwyer showed how he was deeply manipulative and an escalation in the violence of his sexual threats against O'Hara.

Dwyer would write O'Hara messages such as I'm your secret killer, my urge to rape stab and kill is huge, stab rape kill, and most damningly it will all be worth it when I kill you.

O'Hara's replies to Dwyer's texts told investigators a lot about her personality and mental health throughout the course of her relationship with Dwyer. In the early messages, O'Hara was clearly happy to be hearing from Dwyer again; she went along with his fantasies and pledged to do her best to fulfill them. She wanted Dwyer to show her how to be the perfect slave. As time went on, and O'Hara's mental health improved, her replied became very different. She started to tell Dwyer that she didn't want to be stabbed anymore. She wanted a relationship with someone who would be kind to her, someone she could have a baby with. At one point she texted I am a person, I have dignity. Dwyer responded with Not when you're chained up you don't.

When investigators first discovered these damning texts, they had no idea who was behind the words. Although they had seen Dwyer entering and leaving O'Hara's apartment frequently on CCTV footage, they were unable to identify him. None of her friends or family knew about Dwyer or anything about O'Hara being in a relationship. A few friends of O'Hara's from work could recall her talking about a married man she was seeing, but that had been months before she disappeared and they didn't know his name. Police hoped they would be able to find this mystery man through the cellphone itself.

Exactly two weeks after O'Hara's remains were found; police got a hit on the MSTR cellphone. It had been purchased on Grafton Street in Dublin, one of the busiest shopping areas in the city. Police were able to track down the store the phone was purchased from using its serial number. When they approached the store's owner, police were delighted to discover that the man who purchased the phone had left his name and address, but they later turned out to be false.

Having hit a dead end, investigators decided to focus on the text messages themselves to uncover O'Hara's master's hidden identity.

In one of the conversations between O'Hara and the master, O'Hara was congratulating Dwyer on the birth of his daughter the day before. From this, police were able to compile a shortlist of female's babies born in the Dublin area that same day, narrowing in on their man. Dwyer also mentioned in another conversation that he had placed fifth in a model airplane flying competition. Another vague detail about the man they were searching for, or so police thought.

On a whim, one investigator decided to see if any of the local model airplane clubs would be able to provide him with the name of a member who matched the master's description. After making only a few calls, he was greatly rewarded. Police were able to find a model airplane club that met less than a mile away from the reservoir where the cellphones were found. Better yet, they had a member that both matched the man from the CCTV footage as well as personal details they found in the text messages. They had found their man.

By October 2013, two months after O'Hara's remains were found, police were almost certain they had identified the man responsible—Graham Dwyer. Without any prior notice, they visited Dwyer's home and arrested him on the spot in front of his blindsided wife.

Although confident that they now had the right man in custody, police were shocked by the man who had been behind all the master's texts. Dwyer was a 41-year-old man who worked as an architect. He lived in Foxrock, one of Dublin's most expensive areas. Dwyer was also somewhat of a public figure. He had been a guest on several interior design television shows and he and his wife, who was also an architect, had been featured by the Irish Times, one of Ireland's longest running and most reputable newspapers. He was just a normal guy.

After arresting Dwyer in his home, investigators immediately seized all the electronics they could from his home and workplace including his laptop and private computer. Dwyer didn't deny knowing

O'Hara. He admitted he met her on a BDSM website, but claimed they had never met in person. They had had a long term friendship over email, but that was the extent of their relationship. He stated that he believed O'Hara had committed suicide, just like all her friends and family had.

When Dwyer was confronted with the violent master and slave text messages, he denied owning the phone. Dwyer stated that he was trying to help her improve her mental health that was why he maintained an online friendship with her for so long.

Armed with the confidence that they had O'Hara's murderer in custody, investigators started to look for more clues that directly tied Dwyer to the crime. They knew more about him and his interests, and used this information to their advantage. They researched O'Hara's apartment and found a series of small cuts in her mattress and sheets, small cuts that looked like they came from a knife. They also noticed semen stains in her sheets for the first time as well.

The semen found in O'Hara's sheets turned out to be the smoking gun of the case. When a DNA profile was lifted from the semen, they were able to match it to Dwyers. He had clearly been lying to investigators about his relationship with O'Hara, and certainly much more.

Further, on Dwyer's computer, investigators found over 30 damning video clips that proved Dwyer knew O'Hara, and that he enjoyed inflicting pain on her. Among the clips uncovered was a video of Dwyer alone playing with a knife while covered in what was later determined to be ketchup. There were also several other videos of Dwyer engaged in sexual acts with four different women. In each of these clips, Dwyer played with knives and cut the women. One prominent feature of these videos caught investigator's eyes — the most common playmate to feature in all of the footage was none other than Elaine O'Hara.

It seemed that there were two completely different sides to Graham Dwyer: the public persona and family man, and the knife-obsessed monster.

Graham Dwyer continued to deny that he had killed O'Hara. After being confronted with the DNA and video footage evidence he conceded that he had had a master and slave relationship with her, but he denied owning the master's cellphone. Dwyer's denial didn't go far though. Even Dwyer's wife, who had stood by her husband adamantly, could no longer believe he could possibly be innocent after being confronted with the evidence. Despite Dwyer's pleas in the form of letters, Dwyer's wife left him while he was locked up.

By the time Graham Dwyer was put on trial for murder, his face had been plastered across every tabloid magazine available in Ireland. The country was mystified by the man they now dubbed the psycho next door.

It was difficult to believe that a man who appeared as wholesome as Dwyer could have been behind such atrocities. It was the biggest murder trial Ireland had ever seen.

Based on the circumstantial evidence they uncovered, the Irish investigators believed they knew exactly how Dwyer had murdered Elaine O'Hara. To trick police into believing O'Hara's depression had made her commit suicide, Dwyer pounced on O'Hara the day she left the psychiatric hospital. He bombarded her with texts and calls to make sure he didn't miss out on the perfect opportunity.

Dwyer told O'Hara to meet him out in the heavily forested area across the road from the Shanganagh Cemetery, thinking that if

O'Hara's car was found near her mother's grave it would only strengthen the idea that O'Hara had killed herself. Dwyer ordered O'Hara to leave her normal phone at home. Wanting to be the perfect slave, O'Hara followed his orders completely, and walked into the woods to her death.

The two met at a railway bridge, and then walked together further up into the mountains. Dwyer told O'Hara he wanted to have sex with her in the woods and that they needed to find an isolated area. When Dwyer found the perfect spot, he finally carried out his lifelong fantasy of stabbing a woman to death.

After stabbing O'Hara, he drove to another county where he knew there was a reservoir because his model airplane club met closeby. He threw all the evidence into the reservoir, thinking the dark murky waters would hold all his secrets.

The day he killed O'Hara, he went back home to his wife as if nothing had happened. He went to work the next day, and the day after that. He continued about his life exactly as he had every day before killing his lover.

After 40 days of testimony and seven-and-a-half hours of deliberation, the jury delivers a unanimous guilty verdict against Graham Dwyer. He was sentenced to life in prison.

Were it not for the curiosity of a group of men and a dog, Elaine O'Hara might still be assumed to have taken her own life.

Chapter 15

Ireland is a land renowned for its natural beauty and friendly locals. Visitors who take the country at face value might not realize the long history of violence that has played out on its rolling hills and sandy shores. Ireland was the stage for one of the modern world's most horrifying and elongated periods of revolutionary warfare.

Beyond that, many bloody and brutal crimes have taken place on the Emerald Isle — crimes of passion, crimes of convenience, and even some crimes of pure evil.

Made in the USA
Middletown, DE
13 May 2020

94435099R00080